TIM BURTON'S
THE NIGHTMARE
BEFORE CHRISTMAS

Jack's Story

DISNEP
PRESS

New York

Every year, on the last night of October, all the ghouls, ghosts, and goblins of Halloweentown went haunting. Jack Skellington, the Pumpkin King, always led the way.

Jack could scare grown men and make heroes tremble with a wave of his bony hand. And yet, he was bored with it all. Every year it's the same thing, he thought, as he walked through the forest. Poor Jack felt an emptiness in his bones.

Soon Jack came to a grove of unusual trees. Each tree had a door in its trunk, and each door was a different shape. Jack opened the door shaped like a Christmas tree. In a flash, he was sucked down to Christmastown! He found himself surrounded by colored lights, toys, mistletoe, and snowflakes.

Despite the cold, Jack's heart felt warm.

Jack raced back to Halloweentown and told all the ghouls about Christmas.

The ghouls had a lot of questions, especially when they heard about the toys. They wanted to know if the toys snapped, chomped, or exploded. But no one really understood.

Except Sally. Sally believed in Jack. But she didn't like his idea of having Christmas in Halloweentown. It sounded like trouble.

Jack decided to study up on Christmas to discover what it was all about. Soon, he realized there was no reason why he couldn't handle Christmas. In fact, he thought he could make it even better!

Jack gave everyone a job. The vampires made toys. Sally sewed a Santa suit for him. And three ghouls named Lock, Shock, and Barrel had the most important task of all—they had to kidnap Santa Claus so Jack could take his place.

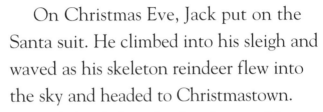

On Christmas Eve, Jack put on the Santa suit. He climbed into his sleigh and waved as his skeleton reindeer flew into the sky and headed to Christmastown.

Jack landed at the first house. He went down the chimney and handed a present to a little boy named Timmie. The boy opened the box, then screamed. Inside was a shrunken head!

"Merry Christmas!" said Jack, smiling.

Jack traveled from rooftop to rooftop. At every house he left behind tricks, not treats—a killer wreath, an evil wooden ducky, a biting doll. The screams followed him through Christmastown.

To Jack, the screams meant happiness. He didn't know any better, because that's what they meant in Halloweentown.

But the people of Christmastown weren't happy. The army even started shooting missiles at the mysterious skeleton in the sleigh.

Meanwhile, Lock, Shock, and Barrel had taken Santa to Oogie Boogie's dungeon. Oogie Boogie was the most foul and evil creature in Halloweentown.

Jack's friend Sally was Santa's only hope. She went to the dungeon to help Santa escape. But Oogie captured her, too!

Then terrible news reached Oogie Boogie's dungeon. The army missiles had hit Jack's sleigh. Jack had last been seen tumbling toward the ground!

Sally gasped, but Oogie laughed. He grabbed a lever, and Santa and Sally started to slide into a vat of boiling stew. But when Oogie didn't hear a splash, he pulled the lever back.

Jack's grinning face greeted him!

The crash had knocked some sense into Jack. He wasn't Santa Claus. He was the Pumpkin King! Jack knew he had to set things right. So, he went to Oogie's dungeon to find Santa Claus.

Oogie tried to escape, but Jack tugged on a string hanging from Oogie's body. Oogie started to unravel. He was made entirely of bugs, spiders, and snakes that crept and crawled away. Soon there was nothing left of Oogie.

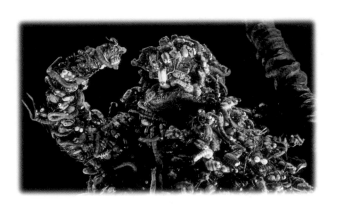

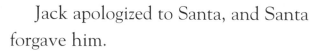

Jack apologized to Santa, and Santa forgave him.

As Sally and Jack walked together, Jack finally realized what would fill the empty place in his heart. It was Sally—his dearest friend. Jack took Sally's hand. Far above them, a Christmas star twinkled brightly in the sky.